A STORY WITHOUT AN END

To

the continuation of fine literature

for readers of all ages

A STORY
WITHOUT AN END

MARK TWAIN

Cover illustration by Joe McDermott

Creative Education, Inc.
Mankato, Minnesota

Published by Creative Education, Inc.
123 South Broad Street, Mankato, Minnesota 56001

Cover illustration by Joe McDermott.

Library of Congress Cataloging-in-Publication Data

Twain, Mark, 1835-1910.
    A Story Without an End.

    Summary: While on his way to propose to the girl of his choice, a young
man finds himself without an essential piece of clothing at a crucial moment.
    I. Title. II. Series.
PS1322.S75 1986   813'.4   85-30885
ISBN 0-88682-064-2

A STORY WITHOUT AN END

We had one game in the ship which was a good time-passer—at least it was at night in the smoking-room when the men were getting freshened up from the day's monotonies and dullnesses. It was the completing of non-complete stories. That is to say, a man would tell all of a story except the finish, then the others would try to supply the ending out of their own invention. When every one who wanted a chance had had it, the man who had introduced the story would give it its original ending—then you could take your choice. Sometimes the new endings turned out to be better than the old one. But the story which called out the most persistent and determined and ambitious effort was one which *had* no ending, and so there was nothing to compare the new-made endings with. The man who told it said he could furnish the particulars up to a certain point only, because that was as much of the tale as he knew. He had read it in a volume of sketches twenty-five years ago, and was interrupted before the end was reached. He would give anyone fifty dollars who would finish the story to the satisfaction of a jury to be appointed by ourselves. We appointed a jury and wrestled with the tale. We invented plenty of endings, but the jury voted them all down. The jury was right. It was a tale which the author of it may possibly have completed satisfactorily, and if he really had that good fortune I would like to know what the ending was. Any ordinary man will find that the story's strength is in its middle, and that there is apparently no way to transfer it to the close, where of course it ought to be. In substance the storiette was as follows:

John Brown, aged thirty-one, good, gentle, bashful, timid, lived in a quiet village in Missouri. He was superintendent of the Presbyterian Sunday-school. It was but a humble distinction; still, it was his only official one, and he was modestly proud of it and was devoted to its work and its interests. The extreme kindliness of his nature was recognized by all; in fact, people said that he was made entirely out of good impulses and bashfulness; that he could always be counted upon for help when it was needed, and for bashfulness both when it was needed, and when it wasn't.

Mary Taylor, twenty-three, modest, sweet, winning, and in character and person beautiful, was all in all to

him. And he was very nearly all in all to her. She was
wavering, his hopes were high. Her mother had been
in opposition from the first. But she was wavering, too;
he could see it. She was being touched by his warm
interest in her two charity protégés and by his
contributions toward their support. These were two
forlorn and aged sisters who lived in a log hut in a
lonely place up a cross-road four miles from Mrs.
Taylor's farm. One of the sisters was crazy, and
sometimes a little violent, but not often.

At last the time seemed ripe for a final advance,
and Brown gathered his courage together and resolved
to make it. He would take along a contribution of
double the usual size, and win the mother over; with
her opposition annulled, the rest of the conquest would
be sure and prompt.

He took to the road in the middle of a placid

12

Sunday afternoon in the soft Missourian summer, and
he was equipped properly for his mission. He was
clothed all in white linen, with a blue ribbon for a
necktie, and he had on dressy tight boots. His horse
and buggy were the finest that the livery-stable could
furnish. The lap-robe was of white linen, it was new,
and it had a hand-worked border that could not be
rivaled in that region for beauty and elaboration.

When he was four miles out on the lonely road and
was walking his horse over a wooden bridge, his straw
hat blew off and fell in the creek, and floated down
and lodged against a bar. He did not quite know what
to do. He must have the hat, that was manifest; but
how was he to get it?

Then he had an idea. The roads were empty,
nobody was stirring. Yes, he would risk it. He led the
horse to the roadside and set it to cropping the grass;

then he undressed and put his clothes in the buggy, petted the horse a moment to secure its compassion and its loyalty, then hurried to the stream. He swam out and soon had the hat. When he got to the top of the bank the horse was gone!

His legs almost gave way under him. The horse was walking leisurely along the road. Brown trotted after it, saying, "Whoa, whoa, there's a good fellow"; but whenever he got near enough to chance a jump for the buggy, the horse quickened its pace a little and defeated him. And so this went on, the naked man perishing with anxiety, and expecting every moment to see people come in sight. He tagged on and on, imploring the horse, beseeching the horse, till he had left a mile behind him, and was closing up on the Taylor premises; then at last he was successful, and got into the buggy. He flung on his shirt, his necktie, and his coat; then reached for—but he was too late; he sat suddenly down and pulled up the lap-robe, for he saw some one coming out of the gate—a woman, he thought. He wheeled the horse to the left, and struck briskly up the cross-road. It was perfectly straight, and exposed on both sides; but there were woods and a sharp turn three miles ahead, and he was very grateful when he got there. As he passed around the turn he slowed down to a walk, and reached for his tr—too late again.

He had come upon Mrs. Enderby, Mrs. Glossop, Mrs. Taylor, and Mary. They were on foot, and seemed tired and excited. They came at once to the buggy and shook hands, and all spoke at once, and said, eagerly and earnestly, how glad they were that he was come, and how fortunate it was. And Mrs. Enderby said, impressively:

"It *looks* like an accident, his coming at such a
time; but let no one profane it with such a name; he
was sent—sent from on high."

They were all moved, and Mrs. Glossop said in an
awed voice:

"Sarah Enderby, you never said a truer word in
your life. This is no accident, it is a special Providence.
He *was* sent. He is an angel—an angel as truly as ever
angel was—an angel of deliverance. I say *angel*, Sarah
Enderby, and will have no other word. Don't let any
one ever say to me again, that there's no such thing as
special Providences; for if this isn't one, let them
account for it that can."

"I *know* it's so," said Mrs. Taylor, fervently. "John
Brown, I could worship you; I could go down on my
knees to you. Didn't something tell you—didn't you
feel that you were sent? I could kiss the hem of your

lap-robe."

He was not able to speak; he was helpless with shame and fright. Mrs. Taylor went on:

"Why, just look at it all around, Julia Glossop. *Any* person can see the hand of Providence in it. Here at noon what do we see? We see the smoke rising. I speak up and say, 'That's the Old People's cabin afire.' Didn't I, Julia Glossop?"

"The very words you said, Nancy Taylor. I was as close to you as I am now, and I heard them. You may have said hut instead of cabin, but in substance it's the same. And you were looking pale, too."

"Pale? I was that pale that if—why, you just compare it with this lap-robe. Then the next thing I said was, 'Mary Taylor, tell the hired man to rig up the team—we'll go to the rescue.' And she said, 'Mother, don't you know you told him he could drive to see his people, and stay over Sunday?' And it was just so. I declare for it, I had forgotten it. 'Then,' said I, 'we'll go afoot.' And go we did. And found Sarah Enderby on the road."

"And we all went together," said Mrs. Enderby. "And found the cabin set fire and burnt down by the crazy one, and the poor old things so old and feeble that they couldn't go afoot. And we got them to a shady place and made them as comfortable as we could, and began to wonder which way to turn to find some way to get them conveyed to Nancy Taylor's house. And I spoke up and said—now what did I say? Didn't I say, 'Providence will provide'?"

"Why sure as you live, so you did! I had forgotten it."

"So had I," said Mrs. Glossop and Mrs. Taylor; "but you certainly *said* it. Now wasn't that remarkable?"

"Yes, I said it. And then we went to Mr. Moseley's,

two miles, and all of them were gone to the camp-
meeting over on Stony Fork; and then we came all the
way back, two miles, and then here, another mile—and
Providence *has* provided. You see it yourselves."

They gazed at each other awe-struck, and lifted
their hands and said in unison:

"It's per-fectly wonderful."

"And then," said Mrs. Glossop, "what do you
think we had better do—let Mr. Brown drive the Old
People to Nancy Taylor's one at a time, or put both of
them in the buggy, and him lead the horse?"

Brown gasped.

"Now, then, that's a question," said Mrs. Enderby.
"You see, we are all tired out, and any way we fix it
it's going to be difficult. For if Mr. Brown takes both
of them, at least one of us must go back to help him,
for he can't load them into the buggy by himself, and

they so helpless."

"That is so," said Mrs. Taylor. "It doesn't look— oh, how would this do!—one of us drive there *with* Mr. Brown, and the rest of you go along to my house and get things ready. I'll go with him. He and I together can lift one of the Old People into the buggy; then drive her to my house and—"

"But who will take care of the other one?" said Mrs. Enderby. "We mustn't leave her there in the woods alone, you know—especially the crazy one. There and back is eight miles, you see."

They had all been sitting on the grass beside the buggy for a while, now, trying to rest their weary bodies. They fell silent a moment or two, and struggled in thought over the baffling situation; then Mrs. Enderby brightened and said:

"I think I've got the idea, now. You see, we can't

walk any more. Think what we've done; four miles there, two to Moseley's, is six, then back to here—nine miles since noon, and not a bite to eat; I declare I don't see how we've done it; and as for me, I am just famishing. Now, somebody's got to go back, to help Mr. Brown—there's no getting around that; but whoever goes has got to ride, not walk. So my idea is this: one of us to ride back with Mr. Brown, then ride to Nancy Taylor's house with one of the Old People, leaving Mr. Brown to keep the other old one company, you all to go now to Nancy's and rest and wait; then one of you drive back and get the other one and drive *her* to Nancy's, and Mr. Brown walk."

"Splendid!" they all cried. "Oh, that will do—that will answer perfectly." And they all said that Mrs. Enderby had the best head for planning in the company; and they said that they wondered that they hadn't thought of this simple plan themselves. They hadn't meant to take back the compliment, good simple souls, and didn't know they had done it. After a consultation it was decided that Mrs. Enderby should drive back with Brown, she being entitled to the distinction because she had invented the plan. Everything now being satisfactorily arranged and settled, the ladies rose, relieved and happy, and brushed down their gowns, and three of them started homeward; Mrs. Enderby set her foot on the buggy step and was about to climb in, when Brown found a remnant of his voice and gasped out—

"Please, Mrs. Enderby, call them back—I am very weak; I can't walk, I can't indeed."

"Why, dear Mr. Brown! You *do* look pale; I am ashamed of myself that I didn't notice it sooner. Come back—all of you! Mr. Brown is not well. Is there

anything I can do for you, Mr. Brown—I'm real sorry.
Are you in pain?"

"No, madam, only weak; I am not sick, but only
just weak—lately; not long, but just lately."

The others came back, and poured out their
sympathies and commiserations, and were full of self-
reproaches for not having noticed how pale he was.
And they at once struck out a new plan, and soon
agreed that it was by far the best of all. They would all
go to Nancy Taylor's house and see to Brown's needs
first. He could lie on the sofa in the parlor, and while
Mrs. Taylor and Mary took care of him the other two
ladies would take the buggy and go and get one of the
Old People, and leave one of themselves with the other
one, and—

By this time, without any solicitation, they were at
the horse's head and were beginning to turn him

around. The danger was imminent, but Brown found his voice again and saved himself. He said—

"But, ladies, you are overlooking something which makes the plan impracticable. You see, if you bring *one* of them home, and one remains behind with the other, there will be three persons there when one of you comes back for that other, for some one must drive the buggy back, and *three* can't come home in it."

They all exclaimed, "Why, sure-ly, that is so!" and they were all perplexed again.

"Dear, dear, what *can* we do?" said Mrs. Glossop; "it is the most mixed-up thing that ever was. The fox and the goose and the corn and things—oh, dear, they are nothing to it."

They sat wearily down once more, to further torture their tormented heads for a plan that would work. Presently Mary offered a plan; it was her first effort. She said:

"I am young and strong, and am refreshed, now. Take Mr. Brown to our house, and give him help—you see how plainly he needs it. I will go back and take care of the Old People; I can be there in twenty minutes. You can go on and do what you first started to do—wait on the main road at our house until somebody comes along with a wagon; then send and bring away the three of us. You won't have to wait long; the farmers will soon be coming back from town now. I will keep old Polly patient and cheered up—the crazy one doesn't need it."

This plan was discussed and accepted; it seemed the best that could be done in the circumstances, and the Old People must be getting discouraged by this time.

Brown felt relieved, and was deeply thankful. Let him once get to the main road and he would find a

way to escape.

Then Mrs. Taylor said:

"The evening chill will be coming on, pretty soon, and those poor old burnt-out things will need some kind of covering. Take the lap-robe with you, dear."

"Very well, Mother, I will."

She stepped to the buggy and put out her hand to take it—

That was the end of the tale. The passenger who told it said that when he read the story twenty-five years ago in a train he was interrupted at that point— the train jumped off a bridge.

At first we thought we could finish the story quite easily, and we set to work with confidence; but it soon began to appear that it was not a simple thing, but difficult and baffling. This was on account of Brown's character—great generosity and kindliness, but complicated with unusual shyness and diffidence, particularly in the presence of ladies. There was his love for Mary, in a hopeful state but not yet secure—just in a condition, indeed, where its affair must be handled with great tact, and no mistakes made, no offense given. And there was the mother—wavering, half willing—by adroit and flawless diplomacy to be won over, now, or perhaps never at all. Also, there were the helpless Old People yonder in the woods waiting—their fate and Brown's happiness to be determined by what Brown should do within the next two seconds. Mary was reaching for the lap-robe; Brown must decide—there was no time to be lost.

Of course none but a happy ending of the story would be accepted by the jury; the finish must find Brown in high credit with the ladies; his behavior without blemish, his modesty unwounded, his character for self-sacrifice maintained, the Old People rescued through him, their benefactor, all the party proud of him, happy in him, his praises on all their tongues.

We tried to arrange this, but it was beset with persistent and irreconcilable difficulties. We saw that Brown's shyness would not allow him to give up the lap-robe. This would offend Mary and her mother; and it would surprise the other ladies, partly because this stinginess toward the suffering Old People would be out of character with Brown, and partly because he was a special Providence and could not properly act so. If asked to explain his conduct, his shyness would not allow him to tell the truth, and lack of invention and practice would find him incapable of contriving a lie that would wash. We worked at the troublesome problem until three in the morning.

Meantime Mary was still reaching for the lap-robe.

We gave it up, and decided to let her continue to reach. It is the reader's privilege to determine for himself how the thing came out.

Mark Twain (1835-1910)

Mark Twain was the pen name of Samuel Longhorne Clemens, generally regarded as the greatest humorist in American literature. While appreciating the laughter and the enjoyment of life, his outlook was often pessimistic, and consequently his writings frequently portrayed this attitude.

Twain was born on November 30, 1835 in Florida, Missouri. At age four he moved with his family to Hannibal, Missouri, which he later immortalized in his classic book, *Tom Sawyer*, under the name of St. Petersburg. By age twelve, after experiencing the death of his father, Twain had grown tired of school. His adventurous spirit enticed him to travel extensively, taking him from St. Louis to New Orleans and eventually out West.

These extensive travels would ultimately provide Twain with some of his greatest stories, as he recalled everything from his days as a riverpilot on the Mississippi to his mining years and the lure of gold in California. Initially, however, it led him to a job as a dispatcher for the Virginia City "Territorial Express" in 1862. It is here where Clemens first signed himself as

Mark Twain, a riverboat term meaning two fathoms.

Thus began a spectacular literary career which would eventually produce such notable tales as: *Tom Sawyer*, *The Adventures of Huckleberry Finn*, *The Prince and the Pauper*, and *The Celebrated Jumping Frog of Calaveras County*. A career that for Twain made work indistinguishable from pleasure, for as he commented that while others toiled, "I spent a lifetime of delightful idleness."

Mark Twain, despite his extraordinary sense of humor spent the last twenty years of his life embittered by misfortune and plagued with bad health. As a result his writing style began to take on the attitude that lived within him. His works began to search for a moral and social reform for society, hoping to overcome what he believed was the selfish nature of man.

Samuel Clemens died on April 21, 1910 at the age of 74, leaving behind works that will as he once dreamed, forever, "excite the laughter of God's creatures."